A New Start

ISBN 978-1-0980-4328-5 (paperback)
ISBN 978-1-0980-4329-2 (digital)

Christian Faith Publishing, Inc.
832 Park Avenue
Meadville, PA 16335
www.christianfaithpublishing.com

Printed in the United States of America

A New Start

Askia Jackson

Asha stood in her bathroom mirror staring at her reflection. There were new notes written with a dry-erase marker that she loved reading every morning. Her mom always made sure she had new positive messages every single day of school to help her remember that she was special and to have a good day.

Today, Asha's eyes started to blur a little as she stared at the notes. Her mind had started to wander. She had a hard time focusing. She was remembering last year and how difficult her school year was. Finding real friends who accepted her for her differences made it even harder. She wanted to stop thinking of bad things but couldn't flip the switch in her mind to turn them off.

"Asha! Your breakfast is getting cold! And you hate cold eggs!"

Hearing her mother's voice causes Asha to snap out of her daydream. Asha knew she had to put on a happy face and pretend she was fine. She didn't want her mom to worry and treat her like a little kid.

Asha finished in the bathroom and headed to the breakfast table. Her mom had made her traditional first day of school breakfast—eggs with cheese, toast with apple jelly, and fresh strawberries. She even had her milk in a coffee mug just like she loved it!

"Now, I know you're worried about a new school year," her mom started quietly from the sink where she was cleaning the breakfast dishes. "But I want you to focus on a new fresh start. Remember: Make friends and have fun. Be kind and stay true. Play nice and work hard. Stay humble and…"

"*Be you!*" She always said the last line of their morning mantra with her mom.

They did their secret handshake, and she ate her breakfast.

Asha had made several friends last year in third grade, but she noticed that they were very selective when she was around. If other friends joined, they would leave her. If they had parties or sleepovers, Asha was never invited. They were nice to her, but she always wondered if they were really her friends. Asha knew she was different, but she didn't like that people treated her differently. She wanted to believe her mother and think that things would be better this school year. Her number 1 hope was to make good grades and make her mother proud. But a close second was to make *real* friends who accepted her for who she was.

Asha had become a professional at hiding her difference. She could do most of the things the other kids could do, and she learned to take the focus off herself so people didn't stare. But when they found out about her handicap, they always treated her different. She noticed the gasps for air because they were shocked at what they saw. She noticed the stares because they wanted to see it one more time. She noticed the whispers because they had questions they were too afraid to ask. She learned to not pay it any attention, but it still made her feel uncomfortable.

Asha walked to the bus stop after kissing her mom on the cheek. She was repeating the positive message from her mom in her head the whole way. She was so focused that she didn't even see the other girl walking parallel to her across the street. When she got to the bus stop, the girl met her there. She said good morning to Asha, and Asha seemed to snap out of her spell.

"Hi! I'm sorry. I was thinking too hard, and I didn't even see you come to this bus stop. Do you live around here?" Asha was happy to see a girl in her neighborhood instead of all the boys and little kids that lived on her street.

"Yes. I just moved down the street with my grandmother because my mom is working far away. My grandmother will be taking care of me this school year. I'm Shan. What's your name?"

"I'm Asha. It's so nice to meet you. I hope we get to be good friends."

Shan shook her head. "Me too! I've been in the neighborhood for a few days, and there are *no* girls to play with! Did all the boys capture them and hold them in their basements—only to be released if they promised to eat worms and pull each other's hair?"

Asha knew she would like Shan right away. They seemed to have a lot in common, and Shan has a hilarious sense of humor. Maybe this would be the year that everything would change for Asha.

Asha and Shan sat together and continue to chat on the bus all the way to school. Asha was listening to Shan as she learned new things about her, but she was also having a conversation with herself in her mind. *Should I tell her about my hand or let her find out on her own? Should I just get it over with and watch how fast she changes her mind about wanting to be friends?*

19

Asha was so busy focusing on what she should do that she didn't hear Shan ask her a question. "Huh?" Asha was being rude and didn't even realize it.

"I was just asking if you knew how to double Dutch. If we can find at least one more girl to play with us, we could all learn."

Asha made a decision at that moment. "Shan, I have a question to ask. Would you be my friend if I told you I was handicap?" Asha was ready to watch for Shan's gestures and see how this would end up.

"Do you mean your hand?" Shan asked. "I heard about it before I met you and just to let you know—you're not as good at hiding it as you think. I think you're a great person. I think you are smart and helpful and really funny. I really want us to be friends, so stop worrying and answer my question!"

Asha's heart seemed to tingle just a little on the inside. She had never met someone who was so genuine and honest. She was so grateful to have met Shan. Someone who didn't judge her for her hand and who actually *wanted* to be her friend.

"I'm willing to learn to double Dutch if you're willing to teach me. But I have to warn you, I have absolutely no coordination or rhythm. So let's see how good of a teacher you are!"

About the Author

Askia Jackson is a veteran elementary educator and a lifetime learner. She enjoys reading, writing, and technology. Askia is from Savannah, Georgia, and enjoys spending time with her husband Joe and her children, Jayna and Camron. This is Askia's very first published book, but she looks forward to many more books to come. Stay tuned!